Give your
PIC1

MW01074428

Dear Parent,

Now children as young as preschool age can have the fun and satisfaction of reading a book all on their own.

In every Picture Reader, there are simple words, rebus pictures, and 24 flash cards to cut out and keep. (There is a flash card for every rebus picture plus extra cards for reading practice.) After children listen to each story a couple of times, they will be ready to try it all by themselves.

Collect all the titles in our Picture Reader series. Once children have mastered these books, they can move on to Levels 1, 2, and 3 in our All Aboard Reading series.

Originally published as THE LITTLE ENGINE THAT COULD™ AND THE BIRTHDAY BIKE

Copyright © 1995 by Platt & Munk, Publishers. All rights reserved. Published by Platt &
Munk Publishers, a division of Grosset & Dunlap, Inc., which is a member of Penguin
Putnam Books for Young Readers, New York. THE LITTLE ENGINE THAT COULD,
engine design, and I THINK I CAN are trademarks of Platt & Munk, Publishers. PLATT &
MUNK is a trademark of Grosset & Dunlap, Inc. Registered in U.S. Patent and Trademark
Office. ALL ABOARD READING is a trademark of The Putnam & Grosset Group.
Published simultaneously in Canada. Printed in the U.S.A. Library of Congress Catalog
Card Number: 95-60346
ISBN 0-448-41973-4   A B C D E F G H I J

ALL ABOARD READING

A PICTURE READER

The Little Engine That Could™ HELPS OUT

Retold by Watty Piper
Illustrated by Cristina Ong

Platt & Munk • New York

"Look at me!"

the little  says

to the  and .

"I can do tricks.

I can walk on

my .

I can stand on a ."

"Look at me!"

says the .

He hops on his .

"I wish I had a 🚲,"

the 🤡 says.

"My birthday is coming.

I hope I get a 🚲."

Soon it is his birthday.

Yes!

The  gets

a new

from the .

The

jumps on the .

But off he falls.

So the  tries again.

Oops!

He falls off

the  again.

The  is not hurt.

But he starts to cry.

"I cannot ride.

I do not like

my 🚲,"

says the 🤡.

And off he runs.

"I must help the ,"

says the .

And off she goes.

Chug, chug.

She looks by the .

Is the  there?

No.

Chug, chug.

She looks by

the circus .

Is the  there?

No.

At last!

There is the —

by the

on a .

The  is still sad.

"Do not feel bad,"

the  tells the .

"It takes time

to learn to ride a .

Try again and say

I think I can.

I think I can."

The 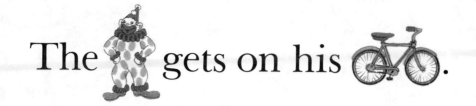 gets on his 🚲.

"I think I can,"

he says, over and over.

Yes!

The 🤡 is riding

his 🚲.

"Look at me!"

says the 🤡.

"Happy birthday!"

say the ,

the ,

and the 🚂.

And then they all

eat the  !

The Little Engine That Could™

bike	clown
ball	monkey
dolls	train

trees	barn
tent	cake
swing	book

duck	window
bus	star
fish	sun

table	dog
apple	truck
cat	bed